BEAR'
BEAR

VIKING
Published by the Penguin Group
27 Wrights Lane, London W8 5TZ, England
Viking Penguin Inc., 40 West 23rd Street, New York, New York 10010, USA
Penguin Books Australia Ltd, Ringwood, Victoria, Australia
Penguin Books Canada Ltd, 2801 John Street, Markham, Ontario, Canada L3R 1B4
Penguin Books (NZ) Ltd, 182–190 Wairau Road, Auckland 10, New Zealand

Penguin Books Ltd, Registered Offices: Harmondsworth, Middlesex, England

Teddy Bear Baker first published 1979
Teddy Bear Postman first published 1981
Teddy Bear Gardener first published 1983
Teddy Bear Farmer first published 1985
Published in one volume 1990
1 3 5 7 9 10 8 6 4 2

Teddy Bear Baker text and illustrations copyright © Phoebe and Selby Worthington, 1979
Teddy Bear Postman text and illustrations copyright © Phoebe and Selby Worthington, 1981
Teddy Bear Gardener text and illustrations copyright © Phoebe and Joan Worthington, 1983
Teddy Bear Farmer text and illustrations copyright © Phoebe and Joan Worthington, 1985

Filmset in Linotron Helvetica Light by Rowland Phototypesetting (London) Ltd
Printed in Italy by LEGO
A CIP catalogue record for this book is available from the British Library
ISBN 0-670-83580-3

TEDDY BEAR FRIENDS

Phoebe Worthington's
• Classic Teddy Bear Stories •

Contents

VIKING

TEDDY BEAR
BAKER

Once upon a time  there was a

Teddy Bear Baker.

He had a shop and a van

and he baked bread and pies and special tarts and cakes for birthday parties.

He got up very early in the morning and lit the fire under his big oven. While the oven was getting hot he had his early morning cup of tea.

He put on his apron and made the dough for the bread. THUMP, THUMP, THUMP he went. THUMP, THUMP, THUMP. Then he made some pies and cakes.

The Teddy Bear Baker put the dough to rise and then he had his breakfast.

When the bread and pies and cakes were nicely baked he put some of them in his shop and some of them in his baker's van.

Then he drove his van along the street. He rang his big bell loudly. CLANG, CLANG, CLANG it went. CLANG, CLANG, CLANG.

The people came out of their houses to buy loaves of bread and pies and cakes. They gave him pennies which he put in a bag hung round his neck – one, two – one, two, three.

Next he drove his van to a house where they were going to have a birthday party. The children were very pleased to see him. They gave him a jelly to take home.

Then the Teddy Bear Baker drove back to his shop and waited for more customers. People liked coming to his shop because he was so polite. He always said 'Good morning,' or 'Good afternoon,' and 'Thank you very much.'

Sometimes he gave the children toffees which he kept in a special tin under the counter.

When the Teddy Bear Baker had sold all the bread he closed the shop and went to have his tea. He toasted muffins in front of the fire and spread them with raspberry jam. Then he had some jelly.

When he had finished his tea he counted his pennies – one, two, three, four, five – one, two, three, four, five – and put them safely in his money box.

The Teddy Bear Baker felt quite tired after his busy day, so he went upstairs, set his little alarm clock to wake him early in the morning, climbed into his little bed, and soon he was fast asleep. And that is the story of the Teddy Bear Baker.

TEDDY BEAR
GARDENER

Once upon a time there

was a Teddy Bear Gardener. He had a spade,

and a fork, and a little

red wheelbarrow.

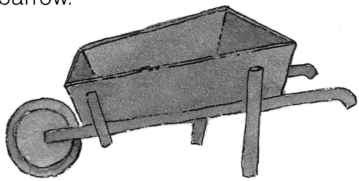

In the morning he went to his tool-shed. He put on his apron. Then he put his clippers and his broom into the barrow.

The Teddy Bear Gardener wheeled his barrow, BUMPETY-*SQUEAK*, BUMPETY-*SQUEAK*, to the lady who lived next door, to help in her garden.

First he cut the hedges, *clip-clip-clip*, *clip-clip-clip*. He clipped the shape of a bird on each of the hedges.

At eleven o'clock the lady brought him a glass o' lemonade and a biscuit.

Then the Teddy Bear Gardener mowed the lawn. He swept up all the grass and put it in his wheelbarrow.

When he had finished the lady paid him five pennies. He put them in the pocket of his apron – one, two, three, four, five.

The Teddy Bear Gardener went back home and had his lunch.

At two o'clock he put his spade and his fork into his wheelbarrow, and wheeled it into his own garden – BUMPETY-*SQUEAK*, BUMPETY-*SQUEAK*. He dug up some carrots, some potatoes and some cabbages. Then he picked some flowers.

When his wheelbarrow was full he pushed it down to the garden gate. He put the vegetables and the flowers on a stall to sell.

People liked to buy vegetables from the Teddy Bear Gardener because they were so good to eat. He always remembered to say 'Good afternoon,' and 'Thank you very much.'

When all the vegetables and flowers had been sold, the Teddy Bear Gardener put his wheelbarrow in the tool-shed and went to have a wash.

After he had had his supper he was very tired, so he climbed the stairs, put on his pyjamas, and soon he was tucked up in bed. And that is the story of the Teddy Bear Gardener.

TEDDY BEAR
FARMER

ANDTE Car

A NDTXO NEXT
NEXT
AND The a
NEXT
NEOT

Once upon a time there was
a Teddy Bear Farmer.

He had a tractor,

a dog

and a housekeeper
called Mrs Muffet.

The Teddy Bear Farmer got up very early in the morning and went to milk his cows. He gave them their food in their manger. Then the Teddy Bear Farmer sat on a stool to milk them. *Swish*, went the milk into the bucket. *Swish-swish, swish-swish*.

He took his churns of milk in a trailer to the gate in the road, and left them for the milk lorry to collect.

Then the Teddy Bear Farmer went back to the house to eat the good breakfast that Mrs Muffet had cooked for him.

After breakfast he let the hens out of the hen-house, and gave them some corn.

Then he went to feed his sow and her little piglets. The Teddy Bear Farmer and Mrs Muffet thought they were very nice.

Next he went to the field to feed his calves.

The Teddy Bear Farmer went to the market. He bought a nice brown and white cow and her calf.

After lunch he tossed the hay over in the little meadow so that it would dry quickly. Mrs Muffet helped him and the work was soon done.

The Teddy Bear Farmer collected the eggs and took them to the dairy. Mrs Muffet was making butter into pats to sell.

There was a knock at the dairy door. A boy had come to buy six brown eggs and a pat of butter. He paid the Teddy Bear Farmer ten pennies – one, two, three, four, five, six, seven, eight, nine, ten.

It was getting dark. The Teddy Bear Farmer went round the farm to shut all the animals up for the night. He shut the hens up very carefully in case a fox came looking for supper.

The Teddy Bear Farmer was very tired. After his bath, he took his cocoa up to bed and looked at pictures in a book. Soon he was fast asleep. And that is the story of the Teddy Bear Farmer.

TEDDY BEAR POSTMAN

Once upon a time there was a Teddy Bear Postman who
lived all by himself. He had a cap with a badge, and a
bag for the letters and cards.

He got up very early every morning, except on Sundays. Sometimes, in the winter, it was still dark.

One Christmas Eve the Teddy Bear Postman went to the station to pick up the sacks of mail.

He pushed the sacks on a handcart to the Post Office. BUMPETY-BUMPETY-BUMP, BUMPETY-BUMPETY-BUMP.

The Teddy Bear Postman sat on a high stool and stamped the letters and parcels. BANG! BANG! BANG! he went. BANG! BANG! BANG! The Post Mistress brought him a nice hot drink.

He found a parcel that had not been packed properly. A pretty doll was slipping out of it, so he got some more paper and string, and wrapped her up carefully.

He took the parcels and the letters and the cards to the right houses. Everyone was pleased to see him.

When he came to the doll's new home the little dog who lived there ran to meet him.

The lady said, 'Merry Christmas, Mr Postman! Come in and have a mince pie and a glass of ginger wine.'

When he had visited all the houses, the Teddy Bear Postman opened the pillar-box in the street and emptied all the letters into his bag. He took them back to the Post Office to be sorted.

He was very tired when he got home so he had a hot bath.

The Teddy Bear Postman ate his supper in front of the fire and wondered what was in his own parcels.

Then he went upstairs, hung up his stocking and climbed into bed. Very soon he was fast asleep. And that is the story of the Teddy Bear Postman.